Lu
Adventure

when fantasy transcends reality

Arianna-Joy

LULU's ADVENTURE

WHEN FANTASY TRANSCENDS REALITY

'Be who you are
Those who mind don't matter
Those who matter don't mind' Theodor Geisel

"I've always had a deep love for books, finding joy in the journey of storytelling. Through reading and writing, I've discovered my voice. I dedicate this book to my loyal and wonderful sister, Queen GIGI, and to my provider, protector, and love, King Mum. Thank you, Mum, for your editing assistance and unwavering support. Gigi, my dear sister, thank you for always being there to listen to my stories when no one else would. And to You, I hope you will also enjoy reading this story. From my heart to yours, thank you. Chix"

CONTENTS

CHAPTER ONE	The Amazing Dance Show	1
CHAPTER TWO	The Class Project	17
CHAPTER THREE	The Sleep Over	25
CHAPTER FOUR	Turning Into Dragons	34
CHAPTER FIVE	Mystery To Solve	44
CHAPTER SIX	Losing Powers	59
CHAPTER SEVEN	Turning Evil	72
CHAPTER EIGHT	Found Violet	79
CHAPTER NINE	The Dungeon	84
CHAPTER TEN	Escaping The Dungeon	100
CHAPTER ELEVEN	Violet	105
CHAPTER TWELVE	Home	118

ACKNOWLEDGEMENTS

Chapter 1

The Amazing Dance Show

It all began on a scorching summer morning when Violet, bubbling with excitement, bounded into her sister's room.

"Violet, why are you up so early?" Nilah, 14, groaned, rubbing her eyes.

"Because it's—" Ding, ding, went the timer.

"See, the timer went off," Violet chirped, already darting out the door. Violet dashed through the house, hunting for her BFF necklace, a must-have for the day ahead—a dance show at school. After a frantic search she found it under her bed, of course. She then enlisted Nilah's help to clasp it around her neck and just as Nilah fastened the last clasp, Mom's voice echoed, *"Breakfast is ready!"*

Their stomachs growling, they rushed to the kitchen, where Mom's signature waffles, scrambled eggs, and cloudy apple juice awaited.

Without pausing, Violet devoured her breakfast, leaving everyone in shock with her lightning speed. As she gulped down her juice, she gestured urgently to Nilah, signalling the need to hurry. Nilah, unable to match Violet's pace, abandoned her breakfast and dashed to brush her teeth, eager to keep up. With shoes on, bags slung over their shoulders, and seat belts buckled, they eagerly awaited their mom's car engine to ignite, ready to head to school.

During the drive, Nilah buried herself in a book, while Violet's grin stretched from ear to ear, lost in daydreams of her upcoming dance recital. Arriving at school, they bid their mom farewell and strolled hand in hand toward the assembly area. After assembly, Violet headed to dance class, parting ways with Nilah. Suddenly, she heard familiar voices behind her and turned to see her two best friends, Autumn and Lulu, waving excitedly.

"*Hi,*" panted Autumn.

"*Hey, how are you today?*" Violet asked.

"Good," Autumn replied with a grin.

"*Do you have your friendship, I mean BFF necklaces?*" chuckled Lulu.

"*Yes!*" Violet and Autumn chorused, their excitement undiminished.

The BFFs skipped towards their dance recital, a mixture of nerves, peace, and sheer excitement bubbling within them. They had poured their everything into preparing for this moment. But as they arrived, Mrs. Ntokozo delivered unexpected news.

"*Attention, attention! I have some not-so-great news,*" she began, her voice carrying a blend of regret and understanding. "*We won't be performing in front of a live audience anymore. Instead, we'll be recording the performance for your parents and siblings to watch online.*"

A wave of disappointment swept through the room, stifled sniffles punctuating the air as children struggled to contain their tears. Amidst the chaos, Violet managed to catch a question or two among the clamour.

 "*Why are we not going on stage? Is it because one of the speakers blew out last night during rehearsal, or the two broken lights, and lastly, could it be the stage is broken?*"

Suddenly, the room erupted into a frenzy of laughter. "*OH NO!*" exclaimed the students, unable to contain their amusement. Mrs. Ntokozo, unable to stifle her own laughter any longer, joined in, her laughter mingling with

Lulu			Violet			Autumn

that of her students. Some were rolling on the ground, others clutching their bellies, caught up in the joy of the moment.

"*ALRIGHT!! 3..2..1 !! Fall in line, class, let's begin!*" commanded Mrs. Ntokozo.

The room fell silent, save for the shuffling of shoes as students quickly fell into position.

"*One more time, let's go,*" Mrs. Ntokozo instructed before clapping her hands twice.

"*Form two lines.*"

From the back of the room, a squeal of excitement echoed through the studio.

"*I can't wait! I just can't wait to see the video, I'm too excited,*" a girl gushed.

"*All right, class, follow my direction while we shoot the video. Are you ready?*" Mrs. Ntokozo asked.

Once the performance began, everyone delivered an exceptionally amazing show. It was an exhilarating feeling for all involved. At the end, Mrs. Ntokozo showered them with praise, expressing how proud she was for their hard work and dedication.

"Grab your lunch bags and meet me in the lounge room for playback," said Mrs. Ntokozo.

Filled with excitement, the students hurriedly gathered their belongings and settled into the lounge room. They watched themselves on a huge plasma screen, their faces lighting up with pride and joy as they relived their performance. At the end, thunderous applause filled the room for a good ten minutes—an outpouring of pure joy.

"A job well done," affirmed the principal, who, by the way, had brought along the rest of the junior school to watch the playback!

"Can the dance kids come to the front so we can give them a clap and a cheer?" requested Ms. Meme.
With heads held high and hearts full of pride, the dance students confidently marched onto the stage to take a bow, basking in the love and praise showered upon them.

"Fantastic dance show, students! Now let's gather our bags and line up at the front of the classroom for end-of-day pick-up," Ms. Meme announced, closing the memorable day on a high note.

As the kids retrieved their bags and lined up in front of the classroom, Violet and her friends overheard their mothers discussing a potential sleepover at Lulu's house. Excitedly agreeing, Lulu burst into a little made-up song: *"We're going to my house, we're going to my house, yeah!"* Laughter filled the air as the girls and their moms shared in the excitement, sealing the agreement with their secret handshake before bidding goodbye.

On the way home, Violet recounted the dance debacle to Nilah, explaining that although they didn't perform live, their performance was recorded for everyone to watch.

"Okay. Now, Nilah, do you have anything to say?" asked Mum.

"Um, yes, I do, well, not really, I don't know. So the first thing is that I have six exams starting tomorrow and 13 more days left of school before holidays begin!" Nilah replied.

"Don't you have a boyfriend?" interrupted Violet.

"No, I do not!" Nilah retorted.

"Yes, you do! And, and I read your secret diary!" Violet exclaimed.

"You did not!" gasped Nilah.

"Yes—" Violet began, but their mum interjected, "

Girls! Please stop your accusations. If Nilah has something to tell me, she will in her own time."

"*Okay,*" Nilah and Lulu groaned.

For a moment, there was deafening silence in the car. They arrived home, and their mother had this to say before they got out of the car,

"Before we go in, I want you to know I have a surprise inside."

Violet squealed with excitement. Their mum opened the door and softly exclaimed, *"Surprise!"* As the sisters entered, they saw their dad sitting on the couch.

"Hi, Dad!" They screamed in unison.

"My beautiful girls!" Their dad enveloped them in a tight embrace, showering them with kisses.

"It's been so long! Oh, how I missed all of you!" he exclaimed with joy.

"I'm on holidays from work for a few months now. So, tell me what's new around here and what you've been up to while I was gone?" he asked, pulling them close.

"We are so excited, Daddy. Come, come, come see the new TV," exclaimed Nilah, eagerly tugging her father's arm to lead him upstairs.

Violet grabbed his other hand, joining in the excitement as they guided him to the toy room.

"*Wow!*" exclaimed Dad. "*That is HUGE!*"

"*I know, right!*" said Nilah. "*Dad, come see my room!*"

"*Did you make a few changes?*" their dad inquired.

"*Yes, I did make a few changes!*" answered Nilah.

As the girls eagerly showed their father around the house, their mother busied herself unpacking groceries in preparation for dinner.

"*Now, girls, whose turn is it to choose dinner?*" asked Mum amid the commotion.

"My turn," declared Nilah.

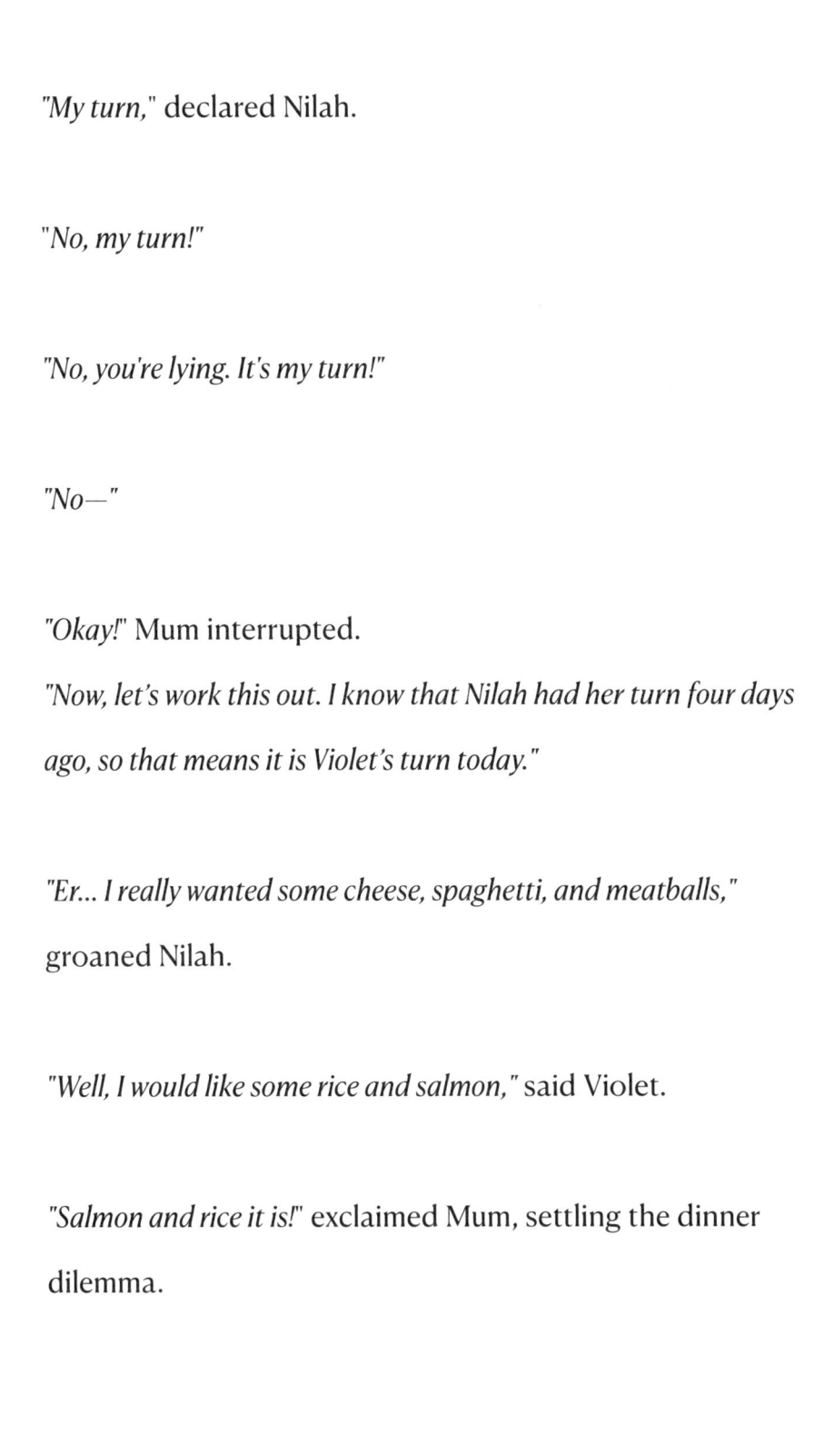

"No, my turn!"

"No, you're lying. It's my turn!"

"No—"

"Okay!" Mum interrupted.
"Now, let's work this out. I know that Nilah had her turn four days ago, so that means it is Violet's turn today."

"Er... I really wanted some cheese, spaghetti, and meatballs," groaned Nilah.

"Well, I would like some rice and salmon," said Violet.

"Salmon and rice it is!" exclaimed Mum, settling the dinner dilemma.

After dinner, the girls cleared the table and put away their dishes before grabbing their dad's arm and leading him back into the family room.

"Um, girls, where are we going?" questioned Dad.

"It's our favourite activity, family movie marathon night!" uttered Nilah.

"Okay, let's get watching!" shouted Violet happily.

"TURN DOWN THE VOLUME!" yelled mum from the kitchen.

"Okay, love! Sorry!" called Dad apologetically. *"Now, let's continue,"* he said quietly.

Violet picked up the remote and turned on the TV.
"Okay, here we go!" Nilah whispered excitedly.

"Ha ha ha, you're going to get me in trouble," Dad whispered, giggling.

The girls stared at their dad and laughed once more.

"All right, which movie are we watching?" Dad asked.

"ME!" the girls chorused excitedly.

"Ha ha ha." "Okay, what movie do you want to watch, Violet?"

"Er... um... can we watch Daddy's Day Camp?"

"Okay!" said their dad.

"This is the best day ever!" screamed Violet.

As the credits rolled for the last movie of the night, Nilah was dozing off in her father's embrace. Gently picking up Nilah, he whispered in Violet's ear, 'I love you, time to brush your teeth and cuddle up with your teddy bear.'

"*Ring a ding ding! Ring a ding ding!*" Violet ran to answer her phone.

Looking at her dad, she whispered, 'sorry, my friend and I promised to call each other tonight.'

"*It's okay,*" said Dad. "*But you better be done and in bed within half an hour.'*

Violet nodded in agreement and retreated to her room for a private phone conversation with her BFF.

"*Hey girl, how are you?*" asked Violet's best friend.

They exchanged pleasantries, catching up on their day despite having spent all day together at school. Violet excitedly shared the surprise awaiting her at home with her friends, and they made plans to catch up the next day before saying their goodbyes.

Violet got into her PJs and hopped into bed, instantly falling asleep cuddling her favourite teddy bear. She had a very strange dream about her and her BFFs turning into dragons. What a dream!!!

Chapter II

The Class Project

"*Wake up, Violet, your alarm clock has been going off for 15 minutes!*" yelled Mum.

"*Okay, Mum! I'm up now! I'll get dressed!*" grumbled Violet. Annoyed, she marched into the kitchen and asked, "*Where are Nilah and Dad?*"

"*Dad went to drop Nilah at a playdate,*" Mum responded. "*Now, eat up! You're already late, I have to drop you off in 5 minutes. You might have to finish your breakfast in the car and don't forget to brush your teeth and pack your lunchbox!*"

Violet arrived at school late, finding her class in the midst of a spelling mock exam. Sneaking in, she asked her friend Lulu, *"What page are we on?"*

"Page 30," Lulu responded.

"Thanks," said Violet.

Ms. Meme turned around and saw Violet. The teacher asked, *"Violet, why are you late?"*

"Oh no," said Violet swallowing a gulp of air. *"Er...um...I slept in... again,"* Violet replied, her voice becoming quieter with each word.

"Well, I'm sending a message to your mum and dad! Because this is the last time this will happen! Do you understand ME?"

"Yes, I un...der...stand," Violet whispered.

"THANK YOU."

"*Sorry, Violet,*" said Autumn as the bell began to ring.

"*All righty, class, everyone can go out and have recess. Except for you, Violet.*" commanded Ms Meme.

"*We will wait out here for you,*" said Lulu and Autumn.

"*Now, Violet, help me understand why you are always late,*" asked Ms. Meme.

"*Well, not always,*" Violet mumbled.

"*Violet, you were late on Monday, Thursday, Wednesday, and Friday!*" exclaimed the teacher.

'*I guess you are right, but I wasn't late on Tuesday, that means not always. Sometimes I'm late, but I don't drive myself to school,* my parents do. Please talk to them, I hate being late sometimes.' Violet responded with a grin on her face.

"All right, Violet, I will speak to your parents about this, but you will have to stay back and catch up on all your work tomorrow." Ms Meme conceded .

"Okay, that's a great idea!" said Violet.

"HA HA HA HA HA. Go and enjoy your recess with your friends now." Chuckled Ms Meme

"Thanks, Ms. Meme! You really are the best teacher!" Squealed Violet as she ran to join she friends for recess, and shortly the bell rang. Everybody rushed to the front of the line, awaiting further instructions.

"Today, we are going to design our own posters, these posters will be based on how you can make the world a better place."

Whispers began to circulate, and Ms. Meme continued, *"Thank you, class! You can quiet down now. I need you to form groups of three for the project."*

"Sorry, Ms. Meme," said one of the students, feeling a little bit guilty.

Violet and her BFFs looked at one another to confirm silently that they would be in the same group.

"Can I join your group?" asked Cookie, who obviously wasn't part of the BFF group.

"Sorry, Cookie; we already have three people."

"Oh... Um, I think you can join Andrew and Antony. They won't mind; they are nice kids," Autumn chimed in.

"Now, class, gather around with your group, and let's get down to business," Ms. Meme instructed.

"You'll need to choose a leader, create a practice poster to brainstorm ideas for your final project. I want to see plenty of creativity on your practice posters. Clear?"

"Alright, I can take the lead," said Violet.

"No way, I want to lead," protested Lulu.

"But I want to be the leader too!" added Autumn.

"How about we settle this with a game of rock-paper-scissors?" suggested Violet.

"Come on, Lulu, you always win at rock-paper-scissors!" complained Violet.

"You can't predict the outcome; let's give it a try," retorted Lulu.

"Fine, Autumn, you're up against me," declared Violet.

"Rock-paper-scissors! Yes, I win!" exclaimed Violet.

"Ugh, you always win against me," grumbled Autumn, feeling a bit envious.

"Alright, Violet and I will take the lead," said Lulu confidently.

"Ha ha ha, you'll never beat me, Violet," teased Lulu.

"You never know," Violet replied.

"Rock-paper-scissors! I win! See, I told you I always win," boasted Lulu.

"Yeah, yeah, let's just get to work," sighed Violet.

A few minutes into the project, the girls wrapped up their brainstorming session for the poster. Once Ms. Meme gave her stamp of approval on their ideas, they plunged into creating the actual poster, working with swift determination.

At the end of the class presentation, showcasing all the posters, a vote was held to determine the best ideas and poster. Despite Violet, Autumn, and Lulu's hard work on their poster, they didn't clinch the top spot. Slightly disappointed, they gathered together for lunch and engaged in various games, quickly letting go of their disappointment over the poster loss.

Chapter III

The Sleepover

The bell rang, signalling the end of the lunch break, and everyone hurried back to their next class. It was time for the dreaded writing class, but for Violet, it was the highlight of her day. She couldn't fathom why her classmates disliked writing so much; for her, it was a chance to unleash her imagination and dive into storytelling.

Today promised to be different. Students were tasked with combining their imaginations in groups of three or four to create a story.

As if by telepathy, the BFFs met at Violet's desk and assigned tasks to each member. *"Don't forget your roles. Violet, you're in charge of the complication. Autumn, you're handling the resolution, and Lulu, you're responsible for the characters."*

"Um...I...Ca—" Lulu began, hesitant.

"*NOW GET TO WORK!*" Mrs. Amira instructed. After enough time had passed, the class was called to attention. "*Come to the floor, please,*" Mrs. Amira called out.

"Um... we're almost finished," said Violet.

Lulu quickly wrapped up her part and declared, "*I am done now.*"

"Really?!" exclaimed one of their classmates, a little jealous.

"Yep."

"O...o... okay," stammered the classmate, a bit surprised.

"All righty," said the teacher, *"now, Lulu's group, can you please come up to the front of the room and present your story?"*

Autumn, the designated reader, began to read in a loud whisper that commanded everyone's attention, *"Our story is called 'The Three Little Girls Walking in the Woods.*
'Once upon a time..."

You could cut the silence with a knife. You couldn't tell if it was due to Autumn's soothing voice or if the story was so interesting that they were all hanging on each word. At pick-up, the BFF only saw Lulu's mum.

"Hello, Ms. Savannah," the girls greeted.

"Hell—" Ms. Savannah was cut off before she could finish her sentence as Mr. Savannah came along, shouting,

"Hey kids, how are you doing?"

"Good!" chorused the kids loudly.

"That's GREAT!!!" said Mr. Savannah.

"Umm, my mum and Autumn's mum usually come at the same time as you, are they running late or in the middle of doing something," queried Violet.

"No, they are not," said Ms. Savannah.

"Oh, okay."

"You girls... are having a sleepover for the weekend!"

"YES!" Cheered the BFFs.

"Now, now, come along; let's head over to our house," said Ms. Savannah.

The girls, along with Ms. Savannah, Mr. Savannah, and Nilah, got into the car.

"Do you want to play rock-paper-scissors?" asked Lulu.

"Sure," said Autumn and Violet.

"I'm so good at rock-paper-scissors that you can't win," Lulu bragged. However, Autumn won.

"W...w...what!!! Bu...b...But how?!" cried Lulu, shocked.

"Can I play?" asked Nilah.

"Sure," said Lulu, *"I've always wanted more competition."* They arrived at Violet's house.

"Why are we at Violet's house?" Lulu questioned confused.

"Oh, I forgot to tell you girls. We're dropping Nilah off at Violet's house first, and then you girls can have a sleepover together for the weekend at Lulu's house."

"Yay!!" Autumn looked at Lulu and said, "*Are you sure?*"

"Yay!"

"Oh, um... I mean, oh man," Lulu stammered.

On their way to Lulu's house, they continued playing rock-paper-scissors. Autumn, Violet, and even Lulu were amazed when Lulu won all the rounds.

The girls ventured into the house to explore.
Mr. Savannah announced that he would be preparing dinner. When Ms Savannah caught wind of this she protested and declared she'd be the chef for the night

All Violet, Autumn, and Lulu could hear were the two Savannahs arguing and bickering about dinner.

"They will sort it out," said Lulu.

"Now, shall we go up to my room and decide on which games to play? Then we can come down and check on them to see if they are still fighting, so we don't starve, I'm sure someone will cook. They both love, and I mean love to cook."

"Yeah, that's a great idea," agreed Violet.

"Sure, we can do that. I think that's a pretty cool idea," said Autumn.

As they entered Lulu's room, its spaciousness greeted them once again, reminding them of the fantastic place it was for play. Quickly changing into their play clothes, Violet and Autumn retrieved their garments from Lulu's house, a convenience they enjoyed by storing clothes in each other's homes. After dressing, they embarked on a game of hide-and-seek. During the game, Violet excitedly shared her dream about turning into dragons with her BFFs.

"*Let's try it out!*" Lulu and Autumn exclaimed in unison.

'*What are we trying,*' asked Lulu

'*The spell, in Violet's dream, remember she said there was a magical spell in her strange dream and we want to know if it works.*' Autumn chimed in.

"*Jinx!...*

Jinx again! ...

Triple jinx!" yelled Autumn and Lulu together, giggling. They all laughed. "*What if it does work?*" said Violet, worried.

"How about we...-" started Autumn.

"Dinner is ready, girls!" shouted Mr. Savannah.

"How about we eat first, then we can try out the turning-into-a-dragon thing after?" said Violet.

"I think that's a great idea," said Lulu.

"Very good idea," added Autumn.

"Ha ha ha. That was very funny, girls," Violet said sarcastically.

"Mr. Savannah is probably waiting for us, so we better get down there and eat. Alright, let's go. I'm so excited to try out that dragon thing," whispered Lulu to the girls.

Chapter IV

Turning into Dragons

The BFFs couldn't eat their dinner fast enough, too eager to transform into dragons. They picked at their food and hurried back to their room, their thoughts consumed by the impending transformation. Thanking the Savannahs they asked to be excused from the table and hurried upstairs to Lulu's room and shut the door behind them.

"Let's give it a shot!" Lulu and Autumn exclaimed together.

"Just be prepared in case it actually works, fingers crossed," Violet added.

'Alright, alright, let's quit wasting time and get to it. On my count, let's go, 3, 2, 1' said Lulu

"Jinx!...

Jinx again! ...

Triple jinx!"

"Waking up in a thick forest, I'm so nervous but excited!" exclaimed Autumn.

"Did it work?" Violet asked as she scanned her new dragon body inch by inch.

"I...I think so. You're a d... dr... dragon, Violet, and you have l... large w...wings," said Lulu in a shocked and awed voice.

"You too!" cried Violet, also in awe.

"This is so amazing!" yelled Autumn.

"So, so, so, how do we get back? I didn't think it would work, I was hoping it would, but now that it has happened I'm kind of happy scared" stated Violet in a nervous cheer.

'Shhhh…listen!' A small and quiet voice shocked them into silence.

"Ask the dragon queen," whispered the ghostly voice.

Violet quickly looked up and around and asking, *"Who is there?"*

"Look down," said the voice.

As Violet's gaze shifted to the ground, she let out an audible gasp, *"Who are you, I mean what are you?!"* she yelled.

The little voice replied, *"I am Gigi, and I am a magical phoenix. I've been sent here to be your guide."*

"I love your wings!" chimed Lulu, *"they're my favourite colours!"*

Still in disbelief, the BFFs tried to stand in unison and fell back to the ground. I guess they forgot that they were no longer human; in fact, they had taken on magical powers in the form of dragons. They needed to learn how to walk and fly, hence the presence of Gigi.

In stillness, Gigi observed the BFFs as they attempted various methods of movement and standing. Finally, she offered guidance, *"Flap your wings, run a little, flap, run faster, take off, glide and repeat... and there you have it."*

"Woohoo! Yeah!" squealed Violet excitedly, flapping her wings, ducking, and weaving up high in the sky. Before you know it, she was soaring like an eagle and showing off her newfound skills!

Gigi bellowed, *"Land next to that funny-looking tree."*

"The one with the triangle?" asked Violet.

"Yep." The girls flew and landed in front of the tree.

"Dragon queen, dragon queen, dragon queen!" chanted the BFFs in unison. Unbeknownst to them and to their surprise, a gigantic rock rolled away from a cave, and a door began to open! They all stood there in disbelief and awe. Did someone hear them? What was in the cave? Were they being followed? Internally, they continued to question what was going on while frozen in place.

"That's it, that's it! You chanted the secret code! Stop thinking and follow me!" exclaimed Gigi as she flew past them.

"Let's follow her," said Violet.
Of course, she was thrilled because she's the adventurous one in the group. Autumn is the cautious one, so she always questions and waits before making any decision, and Lulu, well, she goes with the wind.

Vigilantly, they began to follow behind Gigi. The deeper they went into the cave, a whole new world began to unravel itself. A sea of rainbow dragons, in countless shapes and colours, emitted different sounds and spoke various languages.

"*Utopia, Utopia, Utopia...*" Lost in her own world, Violet began to trudge away from her BFFs, her gaze fixated on a drop-dead gorgeous dragon. It had icy blue-white wings, baby blue diamonds along its spine, and blush polka dots on its belly. Violet had never seen anything like it! The dragon moved back and forth with grace and class, captivating her attention.

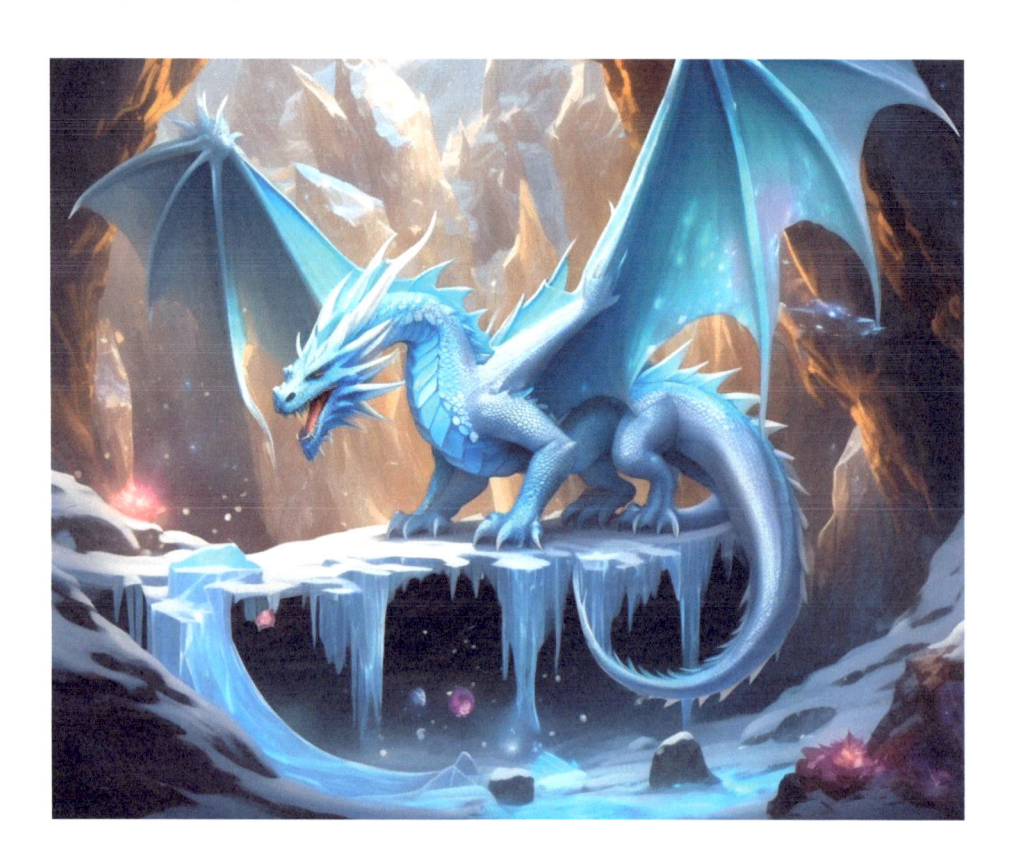

'Take a bow Violet,' whispered Gigi

"That's Queen Blue-Ice"

'Shhhh...did you hear that Autumn? inquired Lulu

Yes, I did that sounded like Gigi, who's is she talking to, in fact where is Violet? Autumn responded as they began looking for Violet.

Following the voices they found Violet, she was struggling to pick up her jaw from the floor as she laid her eyes on the Queen, there was nothing to say, the BFFs stood there in amazement!

"The queen! The dragon Queen, The mighty Queen, Your Majesty, the Chosen one, The one and only, The dream..."

Queen Blue-Ice interrupted Violet, "Are you done? Are you done talking?"

"Oh yes, I mean maybe not I have a few more to go, The great one, The ruler of them all, your highness..." Violet continued

'Points made, I have heard enough! now focus! You must be new?' asked Queen Blue-Ice.

"Yes, we are, but how did you know?" asked Violet nervously.

Lulu let out a nervous laugh. Queen Blue-Ice hummed and asserted, "You need a tour."

"Yes," agreed Violet.

"One question. Do you know how to fly?" Asked the Queen

"Um...uh...yes, we do. Gigi taught us how to fly," Lulu said.

Queen Blue-Ice intentionally scanned the room in search of a new dragon guide for the BFFs.

' A guide must be deemed worthy if they are vigilant, agile, strong, a leader not a follower and have discernment. If these qualities describe you, then step up' commanded the Queen.

A silver eyed, navy blue winged, and black body dragon though small in statue stepped forward, 'I'm Thato and I'll be your guide'.

Thato turned to bow to the Queen as if to ask for approval, the Queen gave a slight head nod . And it was so, Thato was to be their guide!

Chapter V

A Mystery to Solve

Queen Blue-Ice was pacing back and forth lost in thought, she wasn't happy you could just tell. None of dragon dared to disturb her as she paced.

'Attention, attention! All dragons outside now!' She yelled

'Lift your gaze to the heavens,' as if on cue all dragons stared with gaped-jaws.

None of the dragons knew what they were looking at, but their instincts kicked in; danger was afoot. The ominous clouds loomed menacingly in the distance, their darkness enveloping the world below, and swift winds moving with an unknown mission. The Queen knew with certainty that the cloud spelled disaster for their kingdom, and life in it would soon be a thing of the past, with history books blissfully unaware. Though the Queen knew the significance of these clouds, she had to spell it out for her kingdom.

'YES! You should be very afraid, in fact you ought to be shaking in your boots, because those menacing clouds bring nothing but bad news for all of us, that includes our new friends standing over there with Gigi. Those clouds have been possessed by evil spirits and they seek to suck up every single dragon's and other creatures' powers. Once the clouds engulf the whole forest, all dragons and other magical animals will loose their magical powers and our visitor will never be able to get back to their homes. I gather we have eight hours before the spirits are released, we ought to act fast and with caution! Cast all your fears aside and redirect your powers into saving our kingdom! As your Queen I will lead with an iron fist and precision!' Exclaimed the Queen

The Queen gave all dragon tasks to complete, though she didn't give detailed instructions, she expected all dragons to figure it on their own. Lucky for the BFFs they were tasked together and their mission was to save Fairyland

    The BFFs set off for the pond located a stone's throw from the river, with Gigi flying above them. They had to navigate against strong winds, ensuring they didn't collide, especially Gigi. With the winds intensifying, Gigi hitched a ride on Lulu to stay protected from most elements and remain safe. Although these weren't ideal conditions for airborne fun, Lulu seized the moment and soared above the others, a tad risky.

    Watching Lulu being free on a gloomy day made Autumn and Violet follow suit; they had no idea that moment would solidify their friendship for eternity! They were ducking, weaving, and flapping their wings in the cold, windy air. An eerie silence cut through these moments;

tension had to be broken. The BFFs simply couldn't go on as though everything was all rosy.

'*What shall we call ourselves, we need a name like, The three musketeers!*' Shrieked Violet as she flew belly up

"*Val dragons!!*" Lulu chimed excitedly.

"*You know why it's V.A.L, DRAGONS? Because if we put Violet, Lulu, and Autumn together, we get val!*"

"Sure," said Autumn, nodding eagerly, "*that's a great idea!*"

Thud! Lulu crashed into something hard. When she looked, there was nothing there. Brushing it off, she flapped her wings and tried once more. Bang, bang! Again came the crash.

"*That must have hurt,*" said Violet, wincing a little.

Lulu looked very confused as she inspected her surrounds, she was clueless and confused.

'It's was the force field!' Squealed Gigi 'Fairyland must closer than I thought,' she said.

Autumn and Violet flew down to Lulu.
"Are you okay?" they asked.
"Yeah, but my head hurts a little bit.
Um, Gigi, how do we get in?" Lulu responded.

"You just have to repeat after me, 'Fairyland, fairyland, we mean no harm, we are here to save and protect,'" Gigi instructed.

A large air mass began to rotate counterclockwise. As it grew stronger, the eye of the cyclone swallowed Gigi.

The BFFs grew concerned and moved closer to the centre of the air mass. One after the other, they all got sucked in. The air rotated them, spitting them into Fairyland.

"Welcome to Fairyland!" groaned Gigi as she shook the dust off her body.

A tiny little fairy, about the size of an avocado, spotted Gigi. *"Gigi, it's so good to see you."*

"Do you two know each other? How do you know each other?" Violet asked.

"Yeah, no time for niceties. We need to see the Queen-Fairy right away; we have no time to waste," said Gigi as they hurried along.

"Say no more," the fairy said, leading the BFFs and Gigi to the Queen-Fairy

In the midst of this enchanted forest stood a grandiose fairy castle towering beyond the clouds, with a sea of rainbow fairy lights illuminating the walkway leading to the Queen-Fairy's castle. Though Queen-Fairy's castle was grand, its hallways and rooms weren't meant to accommodate dragons.

As the BFFs approached the main castle, a myriad of smaller castles began to light up, with fairies eagerly greeting their visitors. Overwhelmed by the spectacle, they stood patiently, waiting their turn to extend a warm welcome to their guests.

Mesmerised by the beauty of fairyland, the BFFs longed to explore further before meeting Queen-fairy, also known as Queen Live-Anna. However, they knew time was of the essence, and their priority was to focus on the task at hand: protecting Fairyland from impending doom.

Upon Gigi's instructions the BFFs stood at the gates of the castle with their heads bowed as they waited patiently for Queen-Fairy.

Suddenly, the air filled with beautiful chimes, sweet melodies, and bells. Violet felt a tap on her shoulder, carefully, she lifted her head to turn towards the source. Swallowing a gulp of air, she let out a squeaky "*OMG, it's Queen-Fairy.*"

As if on cue, Violet started rambling, "*The queen! The Fairy Queen, The mighty Queen, Your Majesty, the Chosen One, The one and only, The dream Queen...*"

"*Not this again, Violet! We need to focus. There'll be plenty of time to heap praise on Queen-Fairy once we have saved Fairyland!*" Gigi interrupted Violet.

Autumn stepped forward with her head still bowed, "Your Majesty, we have been sent here to save FairyLand, we are at your command."

It felt really weird talking to someone the size of an avocado, but she was still the Queen!

The queen said, *"Follow me."*

They followed the queen to a secret place beyond the shrubs. Queen Fairy pointed at a lone black spot on the ground.

"This morning, someone or something left this mark on the ground. We don't know what it is, but I strongly suspect it could be the evil spirits brought on by those dark clouds. So far, this is the only spot that was targeted, and we're not sure if anything was taken or the significance of it. May I suggest you start your investigations here and work your way to the clouds."

The BFFs looked around, sniffing, touching, and scraping some of the soil in a bid to find some answers, but it was all in vain. They had never seen a mark like that before, especially considering they had only recently become dragons.

"Please, indulge me. I've seen this mark before, many years ago in Dragon Land. An evil spirit descended upon us, nearly destroying the land. Wherever it left this mark, it became a home to conjure more spirits to join its cause. I fear this might be it; we might be lucky if this is the one and only mark," Gigi remarked solemnly.

There were so many questions running through everyone's mind, and the first thing that jumped out of Violet's mouth was a question about a mobile phone.

"Do you have your phone, Lulu?" asked Violet.

"No, but I do have a notebook and a pen," replied Lulu.

"That will do," said Violet. She started to write down the sign on the ground. *"Uh... uhh ... and there we go!"*

As confusion lingered over Violet's actions, it became apparent to everyone that they needed a few more hands on deck to tackle the evil spirits.

Queen-Fairy watched intensely as the dragons attempted to decipher the black mark as if it were a puzzle. "Surely... *there has to be a better way*," she thought to herself.

Perched on Violet's shoulder, the Queen instructed the dragons to summon the Queen and King of Mermaid-waters. "Violet, Lulu, Gigi and autumn I need you to go to mermaid land; they might be able to help speed up this process."

"Yes, Queen," said Violet as they took off.

"Watch out for flying boulders!" Gigi shrilled.

"Flying boulders this time?" cried Lulu.

"Yeah, it is dangerous. You can fly closer to the ground but do not touch anything," replied Gigi.

"Okay," Violet responded.

From a distance, the BFFs caught a glimpse of what appeared to be mermaid-water. The waves were gently caressing the sand as the shadows of big boulders shone across the sands. Not a creature in sight, only the ocean humming its own sweet sea-song.

They found a safe place to land and waited for further instructions from Gigi.

"Gigi, are we supposed to go into the water?' Inquired Lulu

"No. The castles are invisible. We just have to sit and wait.' Bang! A ball came out of nowhere and hit Lulu on the head.

"Not again!" groaned Lulu.

"Are you okay?" Gigi asked.

"Yes, I guess, but now my head is really hurting!" responded Lulu.

"Sorry," said a small voice behind them.

"It's okay, and here's your ball ," said Lulu.

"Thanks. What are your names?" the small voice asked.

"Oh, I'm Violet; this is Autumn, and that's Lulu. Oh, and this is Gigi," Violet replied, pointing at each of them.

"We are looking for the Queen and King of Mermaid-waters." Autumn interrupted

"Why do you need to see the king and queen?" The small voice continued

"Look up, what do you see? What you are looking at is the reason we are here. Queen-Fairy has sent for your Queen and King," replied Autumn.

In a twinkle of an eye, a drawbridge opened up and hit Lulu on the head. Lulu ran away as soon as it hit her head. 'AAAAAAAAAH!' An incensed Lulu could be heard screaming. At this point, it's clear that Lulu will be plagued by a series of unfortunate events.

"Wow!" Autumn gasped.

As the waters parted, creating a pathway, all three dragons and Gigi bowed, waiting for the Queen to acknowledge them. As soon as the Queen tapped on Violet's shoulder, as predicted, she began rambling on.

'The Queen! The King, The mighty Queen, Your Majesty, the Chosen ones, The two and only, The dream Queen and King, His and Her highness, Awesome reigns within…'

Lulu, Autumn, and Gigi had a facepalm moment!

Chapter VI

A Mystery to Solve

'My Queen, would you summon your most trusted horseman to put together our most powerful spells before we head over to Fairyland?' King-Waters asked his Queen-Waters

'Give me a second and it will be so my King', replied Queen-Waters.

A ray of purple and blue lightning flashed across the sea, and it began to put on a show as the BFFs waited with bated breath, watching from dry land.

Whoosh, whoosh, whoosh... out from the depths of the sea, a horseman emerged with a golden object on its back. The Horseman bowed at the feet of Queen-Waters. She placed her thumb on the horseman's forehead and thanked him.

"'The time has come for all of us to leave Mermaid-Waters, are we all ready?" asked the King.

"Oh no," said Violet.

"What is wrong?" asked Lulu.

"Look up." Lulu looked up and saw the nasty clouds drawing closer and darker.

"I hope we can get back on time," chimed Autumn, worriedly.

"We are desperately out of time; we will meet you there," the King barked as he dove into the sea with the Queen behind him.

Gigi and the BFFs wasted no time and took off flying. As they approached Fairyland, they were met by one of the fairy guides who seemed very distressed.

"You need to see this, Hurry, hurry, faster, please!" The fairy pleaded with them.

"OMG!!! What are those?" Violet asked.

"That, you mean those! That's the reason you must hurry, we found many more black spots and they seem to be increasing by the hour and some fairies have gone missing!" replied the fairy.

"Do you mind telling us your name?" Autumn asked the fairy.

"Not at all, my name is Savannah, and my twin sister Amira is right over there with the other fairies. She's the one with a sparkling green dress; she loves sparkles.'

A thud could be heard from a mile away—it was Lulu landing like an elephant on the ground.

"Ouch, ouch, I'm so unlucky!" she exclaimed.

Any other day, everyone would have burst out laughing, but this was a serious moment; they had to be vigilant.

A harmony of charms filled the air as fairies fluttered their wings just above the ground. Queen-Fairy made her way towards the BFFs to welcome them back and announce the imminent arrival of the King and Queen of Mermaid-Waters. In a flash, they too arrived. Queen Fairy took to her throne and began to speak.

"Silence!I need your attention. Welcome one and all, and a special mention to the King and Queen of Mermaid-Waters. We trust you had a safe journey under the sea and we are glad you made it to us on time. It is my understanding that you brought your most powerful potion?" Queen-Fairy remarked.

'Queen-Fairy, thank you for having us. It is unfortunate that we only get to meet under these circumstances. Just like the last three doomsdays, we will fight side by side and conquer without fear and hesitation!' King Mermaid declared, eliciting loud

cheers from the fairies. Feeling motivated and energised, all creatures were ready for the evil spirits.

Suddenly, a flash of lightning shot across the sky, followed by a rumbling of the clouds and bolts of lightning began to engulf the sky, sending fear down all of their spines. Most fairies scattered into their homes, while some huddled together, shaking with fear, and the rest of the creatures froze in place, awaiting the evil that was unfolding.

"*There is no way to fix this,*" a panicked Gigi called out.

"*There is a way!*" the King bellowed.

"*We better get started, time is no longer a friend to us*" Queen Mermaid chimed in.

Lulu, so absent-minded thinking about what might happen, crashed into Queen Mermaid. "Sorry, Your Majesty," she exclaimed.

"That's okay," quipped the Queen.

"Now, Violet, gather all the fairies and head to the bunker. Autumn, you will go with Queen-Fairy and protect her castle. Here is your magic potion. This should shield the Queen-Fairy's castle and yourself. As for you, Lulu, you will fight alongside Queen-

Waters and myself. We will conjure all the evil spirits and trick them into an alternate Fairyland," the King continued.

"Okay, but how do we do that without exposing ourselves to danger?' Lulu asked

"Leave that to Queen-Waters. You will have to trust that Queen-Waters knows what she's doing; she's done this many times before," King-Waters responded.

"What about me?" Gigi whispered, still trembling with fear

"Gigi, you will go back and forth checking on everyone and reporting back to the King. That should be easy enough for you to do. Let's go, let's get it!" The King commanded once more.

As they scattered in different directions, ready for war or battle, a faint sound could be heard coming from the castle. Could that be a fairy stuck? What could that sound be? One thing for certain, it needed to be investigated with haste.

Gigi flapped her wings headed towards the sound. She was the only one fast enough and small enough to investigate. When she reached the castle, she could be heard screaming, *"It's a baby dragon!"*

A crash of thunder shook the castle, prompting a flurry of questions in everyone's minds. How, why, and what was a baby dragon doing in Fairyland, especially at that moment?

Violet rushed to aid the baby dragon, but a bolt of lightning shot across the gates, halting her. She tried again, only to be met with another bolt of lightning. Despite the danger, the baby dragon cried out again, its distress echoing through the air.

"We're coming!" shouted Violet.

"Wait, if you open the gate, a bolt of lightning will strike you," cautioned a voice nearby.

The baby dragon looked so helpless as it continued to sniffle and cry out for aid.

"Hang on, how are we supposed to save her?" asked Lulu with an exasperated tone.

"Autumn, see if you can find a rope anywhere," interrupted Violet with an idea. In a flash, Autumn was back with a rope on hand.

"Found one!"

"Okay, please pass me the rope." Autumn swung the rope and threw it towards Violet, who then lassoed the baby dragon and dragged it towards safety.

"Are you okay?" Autumn asked the baby dragon.

The dragon nodded gratefully and ran off in the direction of the King and Queen of Mermaid-waters, bowing at their feet.

Every other creature present stood there confused, still none the wiser regarding this baby dragon.

"What should we do?" Queried Lulu.

"Hey, your birthday is coming up soon, so why don't you talk about what you want for your birthday?" Autumn interjected, trying to minimise their fears.

"Sure. So, I really want a puppy," said Violet.

"That would be so amazing!" Autumn remarked.
"Yeah, but what if I can't get one?"

BOOM! CRASH!! A loud sound could be heard from a distance. The BFFs ran up to the King and Queen,
"What's that sound now?" An infuriated Violet asked .

"No time to explain; now get to safety!" exclaimed Queen-Waters.

As the BFFs and fairies retreated to safety, a sudden whoosh swept over Fairyland. All creatures began to slow down, some collapsing, unable to fly or move. A loud, boisterous voice reverberated across Fairyland, declaring, "*You will lose your powers forever!*" Accompanied by an evil laugh that sent shivers down their spines, including the mighty King and Queen Waters.

With a weak voice Lulu turned towards Violet and said, '*I didn't know we had powers, did you know we had powers? Not only am I weak, but I'm now very confused. I just want to go home and be normal again*"

Gigi chimed in, "*I know it might be too late, but I forgot to tell you about your powers. Lulu, you have invisible powers, the white diamond on your collar. Autumn, yours is fire power hence *the red diamonds and Violet, you control plants and trees with your green diamonds,"*

A soothing voice could be heard cutting through the stillness of uncertainty , *"Is everyone okay?"*

"No! Who's asking!" shouted everyone.

The voice drew closer they recognised who it was, it was Queen-Fairy. There she was flying above all the creatures.

"Wait what! We can fly; I thought we all lost our powers, remember? How is she flying without powers. Violet wondered out-loud.

"Oh, come on, don't be silly, Violet," said the Queen-Fairy. "I'm sure you still have your powers because I have mine, or mine are more powerful than all of yours. I guess there's only one way to find out."

"*Well, what are you waiting for? Please show us!*" Violet responded to Queen-Fairy with doubt in her tone.

"*Follow me!.*" Queen commanded as she slowly lead them to garden

Desperate to regain her powers, Violet volunteered to go first. Summoning the last bit of strength she had, she did a little jog before flapping her wings. Excitement surged within her as she flapped faster and harder, attempting to take off. However, there was a loud THUD as Violet hit the ground. "*Ouch, that hurt,*" she groaned.

Lulu thought she might be able to do one better, but she too met the same fate. All creatures lay on the garden grounds in excruciating pain. Hopeless, helpless, powerless, and exhausted, they fell into a deep trance.

Chapter VII

Turning evil

Violet lifted her head slowly her eyes crossing path with the Queen-Fairy's, her heart skipped a bit. What seemed like de-javu were old memories coming to the forefront. There was something familiar about that specific crown she had seen before. Queen-Fairy's crown had the exact hieroglyphics as the one in her book back home. Violet began to wonder why it was Queen-Fairy was the only creature who could still fly, what was it about this particular queen. As she continued to ponder another thing stuck out in her mind, it was the Queen's name.

'Hey, hey... Lulu! Autumn! I need to run something past you', Violet whispered

'Does the Queen's name sound familiar to you? Is there anything strange about it? I just have this unsettled feeling about Queen-Fairy and I'm not sure why.' Violet continued

Lulu and Autumn look at each other and shrugged.

'Okay hear me out, I know this will sound crazy, but I know I'm not crazy, ok maybe a little but who isn't. Right, let me focus. Queen-Fairy's crown looks exactly like the one in **'Transformation: Ordinary dragon to royalty Queen Live-Anna'** book back home and get this I think her name Live-Anna spelled backwards is Evil-Anna!' Violet exclaimed

'OMG, the more I think about it the more it makes sense,' Lulu chimed in

"Hmmm...hmmmmm... we have to be sure about this before we accuse Queen-Fairy of bringing evil to Fairyland,' said Autumn

Violet, I have an idea, I think. There is only one way to confirm this. Let's just keep it between us incase we are wrong, we don't want other creatures involved because they live here and we are just visiting. According to the book, that specific crown is possessed with evil spirits, if we can somehow figure out a way to get the crown I should be able to get rid of it. What do you think? Violet asked her BFFs

'I think we should use a Lysol to snatch the crown of Queen's head,' Autumn suggested.

'Ok, if we are sure, can someone pass me the rope, here's hoping we are right,' Violet chuckled nervously as she began to lasso the rope, aiming towards Queen-Fairy's crown.

With a swift motion, she snatched it right off Queen-Fairy's head causing the Queen to fall onto the ground and started shape-shifting into a dragon. In shock, the Queen couldn't process what had just happened as Violet placed her raptor arms on the crown and raised it to the sky. This whirlwind of events left everyone bewildered and speechless.

It would have been the perfect moment for celebration as the Queen had lost the crown, but the universe had other plans. Lulu and Autumn noticed something strange happening to Queen-Fairy and Violet's eyes. Queen-Fairy's eyes turned blue instead of red, and Violet's eyes became black rather than green!

Suddenly Fairyland was deluged with a loud, destabilising roar. Where could that have been coming from everyone wondered silently.

'Rrhhhh! Rrhhhh! I am Queen now! You will all bow before me, you will fear me and your souls will be MINE. Everything here and beyond will be at my command, all mine, ALL MINE!' Violet roared

Trembling with fear Lulu, Autumn and the rest of the creatures realised that Violet had become the evil Queen. It was clear to them in that moment that the crown had evil powers and anyone in possession of it had the power to harm the land, water and the creatures that dwelt within them.

Still is shock Lulu and Autumn weren't sure how to help their friend and whether or not they would be able to return home with their friend. What were they going to tell Violet's mum, friends and siblings. They were stuck!

Queen-Fairy woke up from her haze with a gasp, she looked up at Violet, shocked.

"What happened?" the queen asked, pale.

"No time to explain!" Autumn cried.

The queen began to ponder out loud, *"I had the crown; now Violet's got the crown, so that means nobody else can get the crown."* The queen paused for a moment before she suddenly gasped.

"So, I mean we have to get the crown off her head!" she concluded.

"Easy!' Autumn, grabbed the ladder and climb up to the cloud .

"I'm afraid it's not that easy, Autumn," King-Waters chimed in. "You see, when Queen-Fairy had the crown, it was easy to take it off her because of her stature. However, Violet is a giant among us, and it will take all of us working together to get that crown off her. She now knows we could lasso it; she will just break the rope! First things first, we need to find shelter. Everyone, let's go to the bunker!" King-Waters concluded his speech.

All creatures vigilantly began heading towards the bunker. It didn't take long before Violet caught on to what was going on, and let out the loudest roar shaking the ground beneath them. She took off flying soaring beyond the clouds, in a moment's notice headed back with fury and began spitting fire at all the creatures below.

'Run, duck, weave, run as fast as you can! We are nearly there!' King-waters screamed at the top of his lungs.

All creatures dove into the cave, just before Lulu, who happened to be last, had the chance to dive. Violet landed in front, blocking her path to the bunker. Panting, Lulu begged to be let in.

It was clear that evil spirits had taken over Violet, leaving her devoid of empathy. She commanded Lulu to bow her head, and with fear gripping her, Lulu had no choice but to obey. As she bowed her head, she felt Violet's paws press hard on her forehead, causing her to faint.

Chapter VIII

Found Lulu

When Lulu woke she was laying at Violet's feet helpless and trebling she began to engage Violet.

"What do you want, Your Majesty? I just want to go home, I don't want to be here, I don't belong here, I want to go to school and see my friends, I also...'

'*Silence!*' Violet interrupted Lulu

"You belong to me now, this is your home now. Make friends or don't make friends, frankly that's your business. What I know is *that you belong to me and you will serve me for eternity! ha ha ha!!* Violet let out a menacing laughter.

"What do you mean? And why is there a rope around your neck?" Lulu asked, alarmed.

"Noah! Toby! Bring the surprise," Violet exclaimed, feigning shock.

Her two accomplices brought in Queen Live-Anna!

"Oh no!" Lulu gasped.

"Are you alright, Your Majesty?"

"I'm fine, Lulu! You need to run as soon as an opportunity presents itself!" Queen Anna urged Lulu.

"I can't leave you!"

"I'll be fine. Stick with me," the queen whispered urgently.

"What do you mean?"

"Goodbye, Lulu!" Queen Anna declared dramatically. And swiftly tackling Violet, sending the crown flying.

"Get it!" Queen Live-Anna shouted. Lulu rushed to retrieve it but stumbled and fell.

Violet caught the crown and vanished

"Nooooo!" Lulu and Live-Anna cried out.

"Let's think about where she might go," Lulu suggested.

"Any ideas?" asked Queen Live-Anna.

"Maybe... the flower bed!"

"That's it! Let's go!" As they journeyed, Lulu chattered incessantly, annoying Queen Live-Anna.

"This is why I don't like you!" the queen snapped.

"Sorry, I'll be quiet," Lulu whispered.

"Watch out for spiky vines," warned the queen.

"What vines?" Lulu exclaimed before narrowly avoiding one.

"That was close!" she exclaimed.

"Can I tell you a secret?" Queen Live-Anna asked.

"Sure, what is it?" Lulu replied.

"If you spell Live-Anna backward, you get evil Anna," the queen revealed.

"Yea, we kinda figured that out already, but thank you for your honesty," Lulu revealed.

Meanwhile in the bunker all creatures gathered to devise a plan to save Violet and Lulu while simultaneously destroying the crown.

"We still have the most powerful magic potion from Mermaidwaters and now we get the chance to mix it. We need participation from everyone, starting a fire, finding equipment for the potion to be mixed in and ideas on how we will rub it onto the crown main red diamond. There are no second chances with this, if we miss our shot then its goodnight to all of us!"

Chapter VIIII

The Dungeon

"And my real name is Anna," Queen Live-Anna stated, fixing her gaze on Lulu.

"Okay, uh, let's just go. Let's pretend like this never happened," Anna said, speaking rapidly. As they approached the Dungeon, Queen Anna declared, *"Oh flower bed, oh flower bed, it's time for you to help us."*

Suddenly, two large gates swung open, and the vines vanished. Lulu stared in astonishment, emitting a loud gasp.

"Are you done gawking?" Anna questioned Lulu

"Oh, right!" Lulu exclaimed, hurrying towards Anna but stumbling over a rock and colliding with the queen, resulting in a loud THUD! Quickly regaining her composure, Lulu stood up and uttered,

"OMG!" *"What?!"* the queen inquired.

"OMG! It's even more beautiful than before! I have never seen something more beautiful! Wow, this is amazing! This is now my favourite place, followed by the Dragon Palace, Fairyland, and Mermaid waters. But the mermaid..."

"Okay, back to work. Look around and try to find something out of place," queen Anna interrupted.

The gates closed loudly, startling Lulu & the Queen. Suddenly they heard rustling and loud galloping.

"Um…uh…hello?" Lulu stammered.

"Hello," whispered a raspy voice.

Lulu and Queen Anna tensed. "HA…HA… HA! Got you!"

They sighed in relief—it was only Gigi, but she was too small to have been making those galloping sounds and shutting doors.

"Um, did you hear that?" Lulu asked.

"Yes," Gigi confirmed.

"Just to make sure, did you hear galloping and the doors shutting?" Lulu sort for clarity.

They flinched at the sound of a loud voice.

"HA...HA... HA! I knew you would come here! Now give me the queen, she belongs to me, in fact you all belong to me now! Those who refuse will be banished from this land!" Violet shouted.

"Lulu!" the queen exclaimed.

"What!" Shouted Lulu.

"Okay, um... how do I explain this? Try talking to Violet; she's your best friend, isn't she?" suggested the queen.

"Okay, I'll try. Here I go!" said Lulu determinedly.

"Violet, listen to me. I know I am not that powerful, but I know that there is still good in you somewhere. Now, can we please just have the crown?" pleaded Lulu.

"NO!" yelled the evil Queen Violet.

"YES!" "No!" "YES!" "N—" "STOP!" interrupted the queen.

Violet and Lulu paused and stared at the queen.

"What's going with you?" Lulu blurted out, staring at Queen Anna face turning red.

"I am good! If my face is red, it is because I am very, very, very mad!" declared the queen.

"Okay, okay. Sheesh!" Gigi and Lulu spoke in unison.

"Violet, we really, really, really do need that crown so we can, you know," said the queen.

"We can what?" asked Lulu.

"We need to get the crown. Wait, not the crown—"

"Wait, do you mean the crown on my head? Or a different crown?" interrupted the Violet.

"Oh yeah, the crown on your head," said Lulu.

"No way are you going to take this off my head because it is mine now. Ha ha ha ha!" cackled evil Queen Violet.

"How do you feel about trading?" asked Lulu.

Violet raised a curious brow. "*Maybe,*" she replied cheekily.

"Pretty please, with a cherry on top!" begged Lulu with her cutest face.

"Okay, okay, fine! You can! But it has to be amazing! Like amazing, amazing." Violet retorted

"What are some of your suggestions?" asked Lulu politely.

"I was thinking that maybe I can keep you, Lulu, along with Autumn, in the dungeon," said evil Violet very quickly.

"Wait. What did you just say?" shouted Lulu.

"I just said I would keep you and Autumn in the dungeon!" shouted the evil queen impatiently.

"But, but what about the queen?" asked Lulu.

"Lulu!" yelled Queen Anna.

"What?!"

"YOU JUST TOLD HER TO LOCK ME UP!"

"Oh, thanks for reminding me, Lulu," laughed the evil Violet.

" Queen Anna, you will be my maid! You will clean twenty two hours a day, rest for 2 and back to work.' The rest of you are at my beck and call 24 hours a day. Learn to read my mind and get me everything I need and want before I ask for it. If I have to ask just know you're doomed. If you agree to these terms then maybe I can

consider giving up the crown.' Violet uttered with a grimace on her face.

"Yes, it's a deal," said Lulu as she was desperate to heal the land from its evil. Lulu was Naive to think an evil queen Violet would honour her word.

"*NO! There's no deal!*" yelled the queen Anna.

"*Yes, there is*" shouted evil Violet.

"No, it—" "STOP!" shouted Lulu. This time, Lulu's face was turning red!

"*Um...uh...your face is turning red,*" the queen and Violet blurted out simultaneously.

"Whatever!" shouted Lulu.

"*Wait, did you say my face is turning red?*"

"Um...yes. We did."

An exasperated Lulu let out a roar that pushed Anna to the right and pushed evil Violet to the left.

Shocked at her shear power, Lulu began to panic, *"Oh no! Okay, okay, do what Mum said! Toodles!"* She muttered trying to calm herself, she ran behind a pillar. Ten deep breaths later Lulu was calm. Her face looked normal again. They were all gob smacked, including Violet

"Okay, so can we pretend like that never happened" quipped Lulu

"Um... maybe," chorused everyone.

Amongst the chaos it seemed at though Violet was letting her guard down, Lulu bolted towards the gates.

"Not happening!" thundered Violet.

"Noah, Toby!" commanded Violet, "*take them to the dungeon's holding cells!*"

"*What?!Hold on! Remember, we made a deal!*" A perplexed Queen Anna queried.

"Oh, right." Toby grabbed Lulu, while Noah grabbed Queen Anna.

"*Hey! That is not how you treat a QUEEN!*" fumed Anna making a sudden stop.

"*Get moving!*" said Noah with a quick pull.

Annoyed, frustrated and angry Lulu let out a series of questions, "*Are we there yet?*"
"*NO!*" shouted Toby.

Lulu asked again, "*Are we there yet?*"

"NO!" yelled Noah.

Lulu asked yet again, *"Now, are we there yet?"*

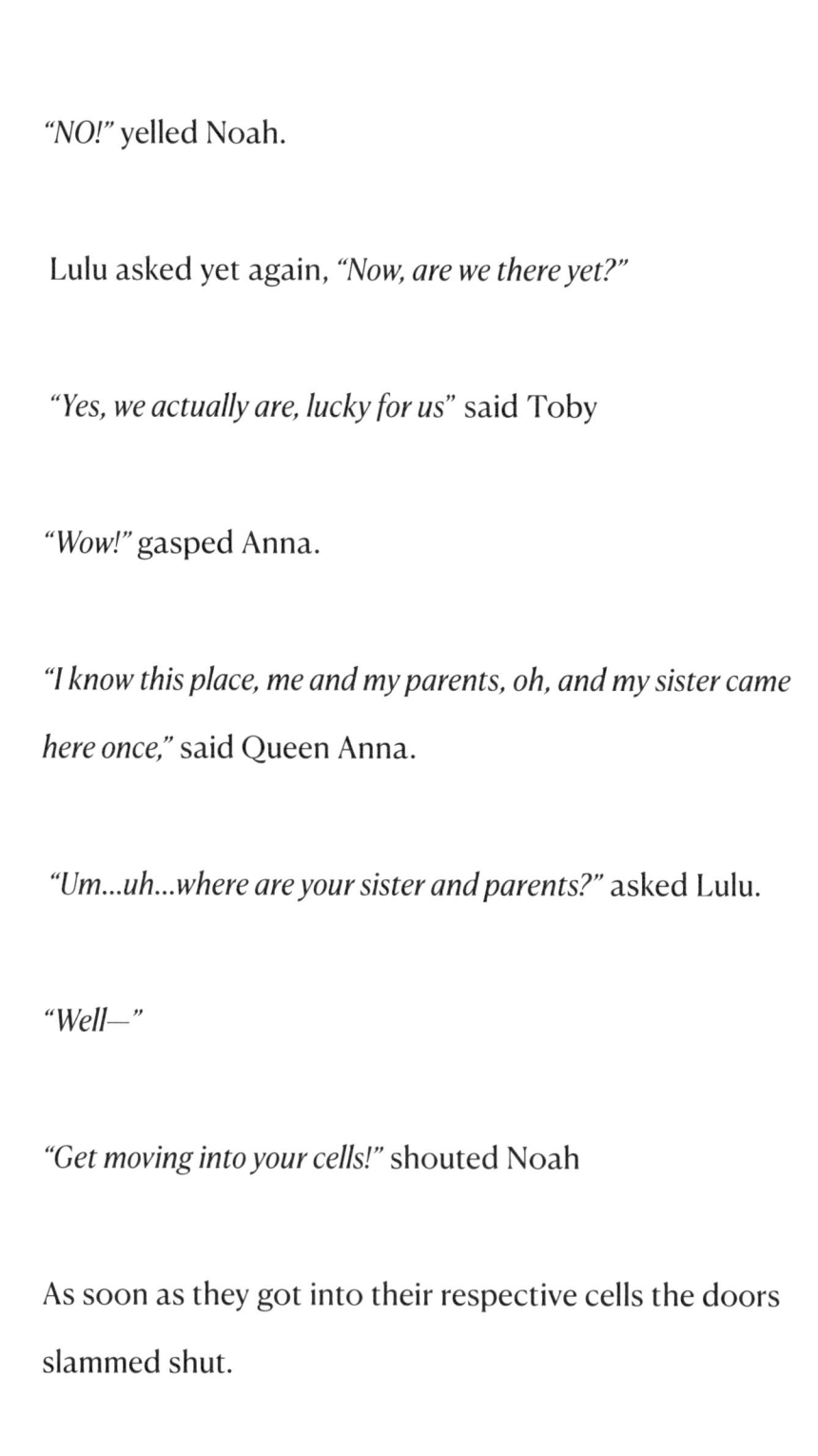

"Yes, we actually are, lucky for us" said Toby

"Wow!" gasped Anna.

"I know this place, me and my parents, oh, and my sister came here once," said Queen Anna.

"Um…uh…where are your sister and parents?" asked Lulu.

"Well—"

"Get moving into your cells!" shouted Noah

As soon as they got into their respective cells the doors slammed shut.

"*WOW! That's a lot of stairs!*" Lulu observed. Her voice echoed through the dungeon.

"*These bars are rusty!*" A voice could be heard

"*HELP ME!*" Another voice

CLING-CLANG! Over and over again.

"*It seems some dragons have been a bit naughty,*' uttered a voice behind them.

"*Um... is someone there?*" fretted Queen Anna.

"*What do you think? Of course, someone or somethings are here with us,*" said Lulu.

"Oh, Lulu, that's just the keeper of the dungeon, Furg," said Queen Anna, relieved.

"Really, his name is FURG?!" Lulu started to laugh so hard that Furg marched up and grabbed her, pulling her against the bar!

"Ow! That really hurt. You are very strong" Lulu quipped as she wrestled to free herself from Furg.

"Don't even think about laughing at my name again! You hear me, do you hear me?!" Furg yelled, spitting in her face.

"Now, nod your head or say it loud! You can say yes out loud if you're brave enough," he sneered,

"your choice" Lulu still in shock was speechless.

She stood up and bravely said, "YES!"

"Oh, someone's being brave," Furg snickered.

"So, who is going first?" he asked with an evil smile

"Hmmm... how about Lulu?"

"Wait, are you talking to me?" asked Lulu.

"Of course, I'm talking to you." Furg assured her.

"We're all wishing you luck. Well, most of us," Furg said as he unlocked the door to Lulu's cell and grabbed her. With her arms and feet bound by chains, Lulu was dragged to the top of the dungeon. As they reached the summit, Furg forced Lulu's head upward, making her look at the dark clouds looming overhead. The clouds seemed even lower than the dungeon itself.

Furg threatened Lulu, warning her that he would throw her off the dungeon if she didn't comply with his demands. Lulu was so frightened that she peed on herself. When Furg was done intimidating her, he shoved Lulu back into her cell and slammed the door shut.

As Lulu sat in her cell, trying to process what had just happened, she was in shock. When Queen Anna attempted to find out what had happened, it wasn't long before she too was dragged to the summit of the dungeon and faced the same threats. One by one, all the dragons and prisoners were taken to the summit and subjected to the same intimidation tactics. This was done to in-still fear in them and ensure they obeyed Queen Violet without question, preventing any plans of escape. Threatening to throw them off the summit was enough to keep them in line.

As Lulu watched prisoners and dragons being dragged one by one out of their cells and returning with nothing but fear, she too began to lose hope. She wondered whether there really would be a way out for them or if this indeed was going to be their fate.

Lulu wasn't sure if she would ever see her friends, her parents, or if she would ever be human again. Thoughts of regret flooded her mind. What was supposed to be a fun time with friends turned into becoming dragons, and in their attempt to save the world, she lost a friend, Violet, to the evil spirit. Now separated from Autumn, Lulu felt alone amidst strangers. The only friend she had left was Violet, but even that bond was shattered. Lulu sat there in sadness, grappling with the possibility that this might be her last moment or the start of a new beginning.

As she sat there contemplating all these things, Lulu began to cry. At first, her sobs were silent, but before long tears started to stream down her face. Before long, a flood of tears overwhelmed her, and she found herself drowning in sorrow.

As she grappled with the overwhelming emotions, Lulu wondered if this was the end. *Was this the fate that awaited her? What now? How would she ever escape this situation? And if she did, what would be the first thing she would do?* These questions weighed heavily on her mind as she searched for a glimmer of hope in the darkness surrounding her.

Chapter X

Escaping the Dungeon

"You've got more punishments coming. Have a nice day, or should I say, decade," Furg taunted the prisoners as he walked away.

"No, you can't do that," Anna protested, but Furg ignored her. As he walked away, a silence fell over the room. It was so thick, you could cut it with a knife.

Ch-ch-ch-ch-ch-ch. Suddenly, there was a noise—a mouse! It startled Lulu. *"Ahhhh, mouse!"* she screamed.

"Shh, I'm harmless," the mouse reassured, offering to guide her to her friend, Autumn.

'*Nope, I don't trust you. In fact, I don't trust anyone,"* said Lulu to the mouse. *"The last time I trusted someone, I ended up here. I* trusted my friend Violet, but here I am, her prisoner. I have trusted so many different creatures. Now I'm having a hard time trusting a mouse, of all creatures, saying that they're coming to rescue me or that they know where Autumn is. So no, I will not trust you. You're going to need to give me more information than 'follow me, I know where your friend is.' said Lulu

"I can understand why you wouldn't trust me. I wouldn't trust anyone or any creature if I was in your position as well," the mouse replied sympathetically. "So, Autumn said to tell you that you had a dance rehearsal and the dance rehearsal was not live, it was recorded for everyone to watch. She also stated that you would completely understand the reference. And I'm hoping that you're going to trust me after this. So, do you know what she means? Do you now trust me?" The mousse quipped as he waited impatiently.

"Okay, okay. Say I trust you. What's the plan? I need to know because, at the end of the day, I still want my friend Violet. That evil spirit has got to go, I don't want to leave here without my *friend. I also want to help Anna even though she was an evil queen, I want to be able to help her. I want to be able to help every creature that's in here. How do we all escape without Furg noticing and without Violet noticing?"* Lulu questioned the mousse.

Lulu agreed to trust the mouse, although it was difficult for her to do so. Surprisingly, the mouse managed to unlock the dungeon cell and free Lulu. Together, they made their way towards Anna's cell and the other creatures that had been imprisoned. When Anna saw Lulu, she was startled.

"Lulu, how did you get out?" Anna asked, not having noticed the mouse walking alongside her.

"Well, you won't believe it. A mouse helped me," Lulu explained.

"Ahhh, mouse!" Ana cried out, but the mouse assured her of its assistance. Anna felt uneasy because she feared they would get caught, as they had been several times before. However, she realised that instead of working against Lulu

and the mouse, they might as well work together to devise a plan to escape the dungeon. One of the birds that had been imprisoned would serve as a distraction. The bird, now freed, would start flying, drawing the attention of the guards. As the guards chased after the bird, they would inadvertently create a clear path for the rest of the creatures to escape.

Lulu and Anna followed the escape route, they encountered a brick wall. The mouse asked Lulu to touch one of the bricks, and when she did, a path appeared. *"Follow me,"* the little mouse said. Lulu and Anna followed right after the mouse, and before they knew it, a portal had opened.

"Don't go in yet, just wait," the mouse instructed. They stood there, waiting patiently. After a little while longer, the mouse announced, *"It is ready. We can now go into the portal one by one."* Still unsure, Lulu and Anna decided to let the rest of the creatures go through the portal before them, just to ensure their safety. Eventually, after Anna had gone through the portal, Lulu held hands with the mouse, and they entered the portal together. As they emerged on the other side, they found themselves in Fairyland, where Autumn was waiting for them.

Lulu was so relieved to fall into the arms of Autumn. As they celebrated their reunion, they quickly realised that their mission hadn't been accomplished. With only a few minutes left before Fairyland and the rest of the lands were engulfed by the dark clouds, they also needed to save their friend Violet and find a way back home. The reality of the situation started to sink in, and Autumn and Lulu held hands for a moment, allowing themselves to process what was going on before they started coming up with a plan to rescue Violet. They stood in silence, contemplating their next steps.

Chapter XI

Violet

" This time we have a plan, and we know our way around the dungeon. We're going to stick to our plan. Those who are not part of the plan are going to stay on this side of the portal. The rest of us are going back into the portal and rescue our friend Violet.

Are we good?" Okay? Okay. Make sure you follow me, alright?" The mousse instructed.

"Alright!" shouted the dragons in unison.

Lulu remarked, *'Are we saying okay a lot?'*

'You're not alone,' Queen Anna chimed in.

They stood at the portal entrance, looking at one another. They nodded in agreement. So, one by one, they went through the portal, landing on the other side where the dungeon was.

"How did we end up so far away?" Autumn asked.

"How did the mousse know about the portal?" Lulu jumped in.

"I forgot to mention, I have portal powers," the mouse revealed.

"Okay, that explains it." Lulu responded.

"Yes, indeed," the mouse chuckled.

"So where can we find Violet?" Autumn inquired.

"Before you answer, do you know how to redeem someone from the dark side?" Autumn queried.

"Yes, it's quite easy if you know what to do and lucky for you I know what to do.

You confront them with a mirror, as they are looking at themselves in the mirror remind them of their true selves, and share a positive memory," the mouse explained.

"By the way, this is goodbye from me, I have taken you as far as I'm allowed!" The mouse snapped his fingers, and vanished.

Lulu teared up, "Oh no, are we too late. Has Violet corrupted the land"

"I understand, but I think we still have a few minutes on the clock" Anna interrupted.

Suddenly, Gigi appeared, wings ablaze, demanding to know Violet's whereabouts.

"Well, you didn't think you could get rid of me that easily. I mean, Violet is my friend now. And yes, of course, I went through the portal. I don't think the mouse saw me though, but he's not here. So, what are we doing? How are we saving Violet? We need to get to it."

"Oh, Gigi, you startled me!" Anna exclaimed.

"Anna, have you seen Autumn or Violet?" Gigi asked urgently.

"Yes, it's complicated... Violet turned evil and enslaved Lulu etc, we are trying to save her," Anna explained.

"What?! But I thought we destroyed the evil crown!" Gigi exclaimed, bewildered.

"Let's head to the Dungeon history library for answers, before we confront Violet" Anna suggested.

The book is called, '**Transformation: Ordinary dragon to royalty Queen Live-Anna'** Gigi located it and struggled to open it, prompting Anna to offer assistance.

Meanwhile, Lulu repeatedly shouting for their attention.

"Dragons, DRAGONS! DRAGONS! Have you found it yet?" Gigi finally managed to open the book, and as she began reading aloud, the tale unfolded.

'Once there was a powerful crown crafted by the Ice Kingdom with the intention to overthrow the Fire Kingdom. Despite the Fire Kingdom's assistance during times of need, the Ice Kingdom harboured resentment towards them.

After the queen's demise, the king absorbed her power and conducted experiments in his secret lab.

When both the Ice Queen and the Fire Queen died under suspicious circumstances, the Ice King seized their power for the evil crown.

With newfound strength, he enslaved the ice creatures and launched an attack on the Fire Kingdom.

However, the Fire King, knowing he couldn't defeat the entire army of ice creatures, used his magic to remove the evil crown, ultimately freezing the Ice King. The Fire Kingdom returned to *normal, and exhausted from the battle, retreated to their caves to live their lives in peace.*

The narrative then shifted to Princess Anna, the Queen and King of Dragon land. King Fire threw a birthday celebration and invited royals from all the lands including Dragon land.

While Anna was playing hide and seek with her peers, she noticed something shiny locked away in a cabinet. Curiosity got the best of her, and she gave in. Opening the cabinet door, which surprisingly was supposed to be locked, she gazed at the crown. At first, she hesitated to touch it, but eventually, curiosity overcame her reluctance. Little did she know, it wasn't just an ordinary crown—it was the evil crown. Ignorant of its true nature, Anna picked up the crown and placed it on her head.

To her horror, Anna fell to the ground, her body shifting from that of a dragon to that of a fairy—a very small fairy, to be precise. But she wasn't just any fairy; she was the queen fairy. The crown, too, shrank with her body as she struggled to flap her wings.

As Anna floated, panic-stricken and in pain, tears streamed down her face helplessly, she called out for her parents. Rushing into the playroom, her parents frantically searched for Anna, only to look up and see that she had transformed into a fairy. Though they recognised Anna's voice, they couldn't recognise her new form. Desperately pleading with her to come down, the parents were in shock, grappling with a myriad of emotions. All they knew at that moment was that they needed their princess to return to them. However, when Anna reached out to them, she inadvertently zapped them with a powerful force, causing them to freeze.

As Anna realised the impact of her actions and the transformation she underwent, she couldn't bear to face any other creature, including the Fire King. So, she flew away, searching for a new home. Eventually, she found herself in Fairyland, where she landed and ultimately became the Queen. However, Anna struggled with the weight of her newfound role as the Queen and the dark secret she now carried within her.

Over time, she grew more sinister, unable to reverse the effects of the crown's influence.

Renaming herself Live-Anna—an anagram of "evil Anna"—she became consumed by her malevolent nature.'

This revelation left Lulu, Gigi, and Autumn utterly stunned. It was newfound information, and they were unsure how to proceed. After much deliberation, they resolved to confront Anna about it. Anna tearfully confessed, feeling overwhelmed by the weight of her mistakes.

Despite their reassurances, Anna remained haunted by the consequences of her actions. However, Gigi's revelation about a potential solution sparked a glimmer of hope. With renewed determination, they set out to retrieve a mirror crucial to reversing the damage inflicted by the evil crown.

As they entered the palace, Gigi's discovery of Violet's whereabouts led to a confrontation, signalling the beginning of their quest to restore balance and right the wrongs caused by the sinister artefact.

Lulu, Gigi, and Violet found themselves face-to-face with Anna. Anna looked at them with disgust, her expression betraying a lack of recognition.

"Well, what now? You managed to escape, and you've decided to bring yourself back because you enjoy pain? I'm telling you right now, you're not going to be able to escape this time. I figured out how you escaped, and that's never going to happen again." Violet sneered.

Violet was so consumed by her desire to cause pain and seek vengeance, she was oblivious to what everyone else was doing. Her focus was solely on herself, her vengeful intentions, and her desire to dominate others. Unaware of the unfolding plan, she continued to talk, unaware of the impending distraction. Sensing an opportunity, Lulu signalled to the others that she would try to distract Violet while Anna held up the mirror she had been hiding. As Lulu engaged Violet, Anna swiftly held the mirror in front of Violet's face. Before Violet could comprehend what was happening, she found herself staring at her own reflection in the mirror. Stunned by her own reflection she stood still.

Taking a moment to compose herself, Lulu began to speak to her friend.

"Violet, you are more than just good; you are great and awesome. You're not only my best friend but Autumn's too. Remember our sleepover? The night we transformed into dragons? And the times I struggled to fly?" Lulu chuckled at the memories.

"Violet, you're an incredible friend."

Suddenly, there was a tremendous BOOM! Miraculously, Violet fell to the ground, loosing the crown and slowly returned to her true self, a portal appeared and sucked the crown into it restoring the kingdom and the dark clouds dissipating into the sky.

"Violet! Lulu! Autumn! Everything is back to normal!" exclaimed Anna, filled with relief.

"Yes, Queen Anna, we did it!" cheered Lulu, sharing in the victory.

"But wait, who's Queen Anna? Why does she... look so much like Queen Live-Anna?" asked Violet, confused.

"Oh, about that, my real name is Anna. So, do you want the whole story?" the queen asked.

"YEAH!" said the Violet eagerly.

"Okay, so it started on a sunny day. I was only 4—almost 5— and I was running along the grass with my parents. We were playing hide and seek. I went hiding and saw something shiny on the ground. I picked it up, and my parents came running as they heard me crying.

They saw me floating on a cloud and called for me to come down. I reached out to them, but there was a zap, and my parents froze. I descended from the cloud, crying and waiting for a response from them.

In a moment, I realised that I was now Queen-Fairy. I became consumed by darkness, unable to remove the crown or stop turning people into my slaves. And that is the story," Anna concluded.

"If you want the whole story, I mean the real truth, please go to the Dragon History Library," added Gigi.

The dragons all stared at Anna in shock.

"What?!" they all exclaimed.

"I know! But do not tell anyone, or else!" the queen warned sternly.

"Okay, we have to get back now," Autumn suggested.

"What will your parents say, Lulu?"

"Oh, there is one way you can get back quickly. You just have to face that mirror and ask it where you would like to go. Oh, and time froze in your world," Queen Anna explained.

"Well, that's great," said Autumn, feeling relieved.

Chapter XII

Home

"Okay, BFFs head home, and thank you for saving our worlds" remarked Anna.

A baby dragon approached Violet timidly.

"Are you the dragons that saved the kingdom?" it asked softly.

"You bet we are!" exclaimed Lulu proudly.

"Well, can you please follow me?" requested the baby dragon.

"Um, sure, I mean, time is frozen in our world," replied Lulu hesitantly.

They followed the baby dragon outside, where they were met with a heartwarming surprise.

"*Surprise!*" All the dragons had organised a party to thank them for saving the kingdom.

"*OMG! Thank you, everyone!*" the BFFs exclaimed gratefully.

After some time, Violet announced, "*Okay, dragons, we have to get back!*" "*Goodbye, dragons!*" the BFFs bid farewell.

With a chorus of roars, the dragons watched as the girls walked into the mirror, POOF! They disappeared back into the human world.

"*Girls, would you like some dessert?*" Mr. Savannah asked.

"*You girls okay?*" Ms. Savannah questioned when they didn't reply immediately.

"*Um, yeah, we just had a...*" Lulu hesitated.

"Oh, that's great. Now, who wants ice cream with chocolate donuts?"

There was silence, and then... *"ME!"* the girls shouted happily together. They hurried down to the kitchen and settled into their seats.

Lulu's dad inquired, *"What do we want to eat today, ladies?"*

"May I have vanilla ice cream with two mini chocolate mint donuts?" requested Lulu.

"May I have mint ice cream with a chocolate donut, please?" asked Violet politely.

"And can I please have lemon sorbet and a chocolate donut, pretty please, with a cherry on top?" added Autumn.

Ms. Savannah went to the convenience store a few blocks away to fulfil their orders.

Woof! woof! barked a Spot, their dog.

"*Spot!*" yelled Lulu excitedly as their dog entered the room.

"*Hi, Spot!*" "*I'm home!*" announced Lulu's mum as she entered the house. They enjoyed their treats and played with Spot before changing into their pyjamas.

"*Off to bed now,*" instructed Lulu's dad.

"*Night, girls,*" bid Violet.

"*Good night, everyone!*" said Lulu.

"*Night,*" echoed Autumn.

As Lulu's parents closed the door, a small whisper filled the room, "*Make sure you don't tell anyone about the adventure!*"

'Who's that,' the BFF's questioned in unison!

ACKNOWLEDGEMENTS

Dear reader, thank you so much for taking the time to explore this captivating story! I poured my heart into it, fuelled by my passion for reading and writing. I'm thrilled to share it with you, and I truly hope you enjoy it as much as I enjoyed crafting it. It's a testament to my dedication to the written word, and I'm proud to have completed it.

Chix   Gigi

Made in the USA
Columbia, SC
27 May 2024